STABAT MATER DOLOROSA

FOR

EIGHT VOICES

BY

PALESTRINA

GW00402485

EDITED AND ARRANGED FOR MODERN USE BY

HENRY WASHINGTON

—————

Duration of performance 25 minutes

—————

CHESTER MUSIC

(A division of Music Sales Limited)
8/9 Frith Street, London W1V 5TZ

PREFACE

The freely-composed liturgical Sequences which flourished from about the eleventh century onwards evolved from the earlier practice of "troping" the Chants of the Ordinarium. The primitive tropes of about 900 A.D.—possibly earlier—consisted of "farcing" or filling out the melismata of certain sections of the Gregorian Mass chants with syllabic verbal texts mostly in honour of the Deity or of the Blessed Virgin. Vestiges of such interpolation in the *Kyrie eleison* may be observed in the titles of some of the Mass Ordinaries of the present Kyriale, e.g., in *Kyrie fons bonitatis, Cunctipotens Genitor Deus, Stelliferi Conditor orbis*, etc.*

The term Sequence was always confined to the farcing of the Alleluia jubilus which follows the Alleluia verse. It is on record that the Sequence eventually displaced the Alleluia verse and developed into a free composition. France seems to have had a long history of the Sequence in which rhyming stanzas were widely employed.† The art and practice of these lengthy and often beautiful syllabic compositions became widespread throughout Christendom, particularly between the eleventh and thirteenth centuries. But ecclesiastical authority came to believe that the length and beauty of these appended hymns detracted from the prayerfulness and meaning of the traditional Gregorian chants. Hence the Council of Trent (1545–1563) expunged all but four of the then existing Sequences, viz. the *Victimae Paschale* of Easter, *Veni Sancte Spiritus* of Pentecost, *Lauda Sion* of Corpus Christi and *Dies Irae* of the Missa pro Defunctis.

However, the *Stabat Mater Dolorosa*, attributed to the Franciscan Jacopone da Todi, (*circa* 1228–1306) was restored to the Graduale Romanum for the Feast of Our Lady of the Seven Dolours (15th September) in 1727, with a slightly modified verbal text.

In the present climate of liturgical revision there is little possibility of performing Palestrina's beautiful setting of *Stabat Mater Dolorosa* in its proper liturgical position. It is indeed unlikely that this work has ever been performed in its entirety during the celebration of Holy Mass. It is known that the first part only was sung, slowly and reverently, at the Offertory in St. Peter's by the Papal choir during Holy Week while the action of the Mass was deliberately suspended.

An extra-liturgical performance of this masterpiece is, of course, suitable at any time, preferably during Holy Week, e.g., the Holy Communion on Good Friday. I have, therefore, thought fit to retain the original verbal text as set by Palestrina so that rhyme and metre remain perfectly matched.

This present edition is based upon the transcription in Breitkopf & Härtel's collection of Palestrina's complete works by Haberl and Espagne. I have halved the original note-values to conform to present-day acceptance of the crotchet as the normal unit of Time. The ictus sign $\wr$, a note with a short vertical stroke placed above or below it, is freely used in this edition with the two-fold object of defending verbal rhythm against the accentual power associated with the modern bar-line and of defining the true agogic accent where an original long note has been replaced by two tied notes of shorter duration. This device should serve to protect the rhythmic subtleties of this most expressive example of Renaissance musical art.

I have decided to reprint this work in the original natural scale. It will be observed from the prefixed voice-ranges that the two choruses are equal in pitch. It is worth mentioning, however, that the two Altus parts are basically within the octave C to C, the only deviation being a low B in the First Chorus and a single dip to low A in the cadence of *Nati poenas inclyti* in the Second Chorus Altus part.

Another point of practical interest is that the tessitura of the Cantus of the First Choir stands higher than that of the Second Choir. This is also true of the first Chorus Tenor part. As the piece is *A Cappella* and continuous there is then no problem in setting the pitch a semitone or even a whole tone lower if local conditions seem to demand it.

Henry Washington, K.S.G.

Amersham
Feast of Our Lady of the Seven Dolours.

15*th September*, 1973.

* Complete examples of these tropes are to be found in the Plainsong and Mediaeval Music Society's facsimile reproduction of the Antiphonale Sarisburiense.
† The above notes offer no more than a brief introduction to this early period of Christian music in which uncertainties still abound. For a comprehensive study refer to Jacques Handschin: Trope, Sequence and Conductus, in Volume 11 of the New Oxford History of Music.

STABAT MATER DOLOROSA

PALESTRINA
edited by
HENRY WASHINGTON

4

10

Dum - pen-dé-bat ___ Fí - li - us.

Dum - pen-dé-bat Fí - li - us. ___

Dum - pen-dé-bat Fí - li - us.

Dum - pen-dé-bat Fí - li - us. ___

10

- cem la - cri - mó - sa, Cu - jus

- cem la - cri - mó - sa, Cu - jus

- cem la - cri - mó - sa, Cu - jus

- cem la - cri - mó - sa, Cu - jus

10

f

poco rit.

mf

a tempo

6

be - ne - dí - cta Ma - ter U - ni - gé - ni - ti! et__ do - lé -

be - ne - dí - cta Ma - ter U - ni - gé - ni - ti! et__ do - lé -

be - ne - dí - cta Ma - ter U - ni - gé - ni - ti! et__ do - lé -

be - ne - dí - cta Ma - ter U - ni - gé - ni - ti! et__ do - lé -

Quae mœ - ré - bat,

Quae mœ - ré - bat,

Quae mœ - ré - bat,

Quae mœ - ré - bat,

poco rit.   *a tempo*
soli
f

In tan-to sup-plí - - - ci - o?

In tan - to sup - plí - ci - o?

In tan-to sup-plí - - - ci - o?

In tan-to sup-plí - ci - o?

-trem si vi -dé - ret   Quis non

-trem si vi -dé - ret   Quis non

- trem si vi -dé - ret   Quis non

-trem si vi -dé - ret   Quis non

Tutti
mf   *p* soli

14

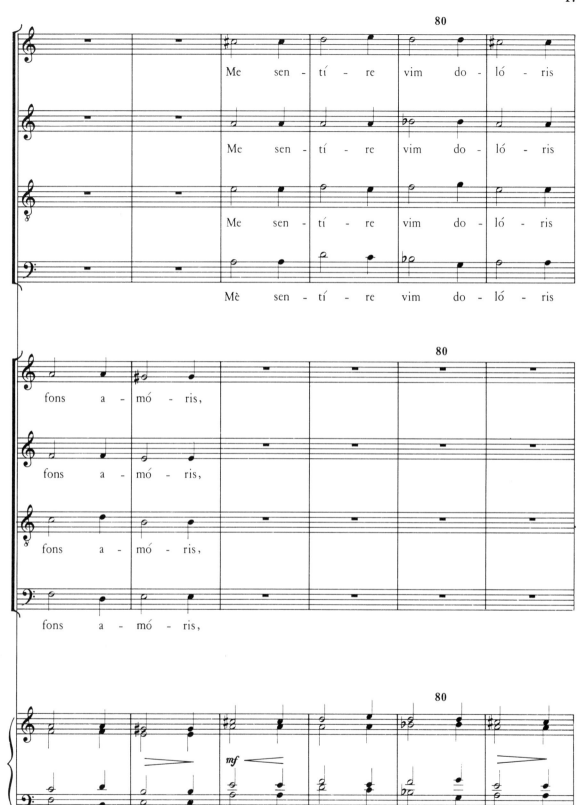

18

Fac, ut te - cum lú - ge - am.

Fac, ut te - cum lú - ge - am.

Fac, ut te - cum lú - ge - am.

Fac, ut te - cum lú - ge - am.

Fac ut ár - de - at cor me - um In a -

Fac ut ár - de - at cor me - um In a -

Fac ut ár - de - at cor me - um In a -

Fac ut ár - de - at cor me - um In a -

22

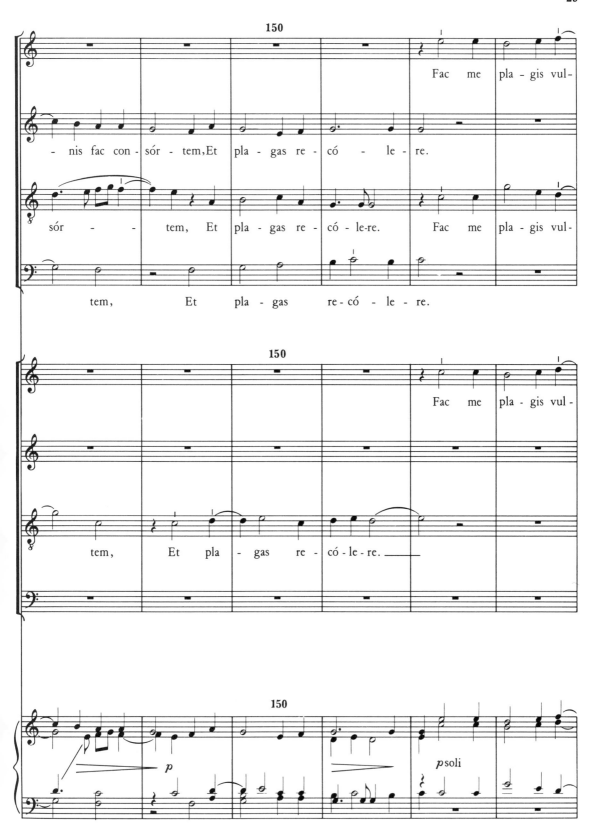

Soon the music has to go
out of print . . . .

Printed by Caligraving Limited Thetford Norf